Stage 12

KT-198-951

The Witch-Baby

Cara Lockhart Smith

Illustrated by Bridget MacKeith

TIGERS

Andersen Press · London

First published in 1998 by
Andersen Press Limited,
20 Vauxhall Bridge Road, London SW1V 2SA

Text © 1998 by Cara Lockhart Smith
Illustrations © 1998 by Bridget MacKeith

The rights of Cara Lockhart Smith and Bridget
MacKeith to be identified as the author and
illustrator of this work have been asserted by them in
accordance with the Copyright, Designs and Patents
Act, 1988.

British Library Cataloguing in Publication Data
available
ISBN 0 86264 800 9

Phototypeset by Intype London Ltd
Printed and bound in Great Britain
by the Guernsey Press Co. Ltd., Guernsey, Channel Islands

Contents

1
The Alarm Clock

Sophie Starling lived in a small house in Cairo Street, just behind Ellison's Scrapyard. She had a room all to herself, a beautiful room with an old brass bed, a duvet with stars all over it, and two big pillows.

The bed was so comfy that in the mornings Sophie stayed snuggled up inside it, sound asleep, instead of getting up in time to go to school.

Her dad slept in late, and her mother did nights at the hospital, so often there was nobody around in the morning to give Sophie a nudge and a shake and tell her to get up. So almost every morning she was late for school!

Then one evening, Halloween it was, Sophie found an old alarm clock at the back of a drawer in the kitchen. '*This* will wake me up in time for school!' she said. She set the alarm for eight o'clock and put it beside her bed.

Now this clock, when you wound it
up, had a loud and confident *tick-tock*.
But unfortunately, the thing was
BONKERS! It ticked away quite
happily but *much too fast*. So next
morning, when the alarm went off

PRIIIIIINNNGGG!!!!!!

in Sophie's ear, it
wasn't eight at all, but
still only six in the morning.

Sophie blinked the sleep out of her eyes and sat up.

'It's a bit dark!' she said, surprised. Nevertheless, she jumped up, pulled on her school clothes, and ran downstairs, grabbed herself a bottle of Coke and a piece of fruit cake, and rushed out of the house. The milkman was delivering bottles all down the street.

'That milkman is a bit late,' thought Sophie. 'For a milkman, that is. But I'm on time!'

The moon was still shining in the dark blue sky. It was a cold November morning.

Sophie walked to the end of Cairo Street, and then turned into the road that ran along beside Ellison's Scrapyard.

The scrapyard was piled
with heaps of metal that glinted under
the moonlight. Sophie shivered. She
began to run, and then she stopped
stock-still.

The gate to the scrapyard was open,
and there in the gateway, propped up
against a small pile of bricks, was a . . .

BABY!

A very peculiar baby indeed!

2
The Witch-Baby

Sophie didn't know that much about
babies. All the same she could see this
one was a bit odd. It had pale skin with
a greenish tinge, and big goblin eyes
like a grasshopper. It was wrapped in
a long green cobwebby shawl, and
perched on its head was a small
pointed hat.

The baby opened its mouth and
said:

Grubba digrubbadiabracadab

Then it stopped its racket abruptly and gazed at Sophie.

Sophie stared back at the baby. What on earth was it doing all by itself, leaning up against a pile of bricks at the entrance to Ellison's Scrapyard? She jiggled from foot to foot.

'Hello, baby. Shouldn't you be safe at home?'

'Leff me,' said the baby. It spoke well for its age. 'Pick m'yup she will, at minnight.'

'Who will?' asked Sophie, shifting herself a little nearer.

The baby lifted its arms up and waggled them towards her.

'Witch-Mummy!' it said.

'What do you mean, which mummy?
How should I know which mummy?'

'*Witch*-Mummy. My mummy. My
mummy the witch,' said the baby, a
little sadly and crossly at the same
time. 'Me is loss, me is cold, pick
m'yup!' said the baby.

Sophie thought for a moment, then
she picked up the baby, who was as
light as a pillow though slightly
slippery. The baby looked up at her
with its big goblin eyes and gave her a
little shivery grin.

'You're a Witch-Baby!' said Sophie.
'I can't leave you sitting here next to
a pile of bricks. You'd better come
along with me, and I'll try my best to
look after you until your mummy
comes back!'

She hoiked the baby under her arm,
and ran off to school. Of course, when
she got there, the school clock said half
past six!

'That stupid old alarm clock must have been haywire!' thought Sophie. 'Oh well, if I hadn't been early, then I wouldn't have found the baby, and then it might really have got into trouble, and never seen its mother again.'

The baby blinked at her.

'Now listen,' said Sophie, 'I'm going to smuggle you into lessons. Our Mrs Larkin is a bit short-sighted and ever so vague, so she probably won't notice

you're a bit strange. But if she does,
I'll just pretend you're my favourite
toy that I've brought in for our painting
project. I'll give you back to your
mummy at midnight. We'll wait for her
outside the scrapyard. Until then, just
try and be a nice quiet baby, and don't
cause trouble, okay?'

'Kay O,' said the baby.

Sophie sat down with the baby in
the empty bike shed, and they both
snoozed off.

Round about a quarter to nine, everyone started arriving for school. Sophie's friends came crowding round her, goggling at the baby:
'Where'd you get it?'
'D'ya wanna do a swap?'
'It looks really extra-terrestrial, that does.'
'What on earth is it, Sophie?'

'Ask me no questions and I'll tell
you no lies,' said Sophie.

She got up, wrapped the cobwebby
shawl tightly round the
baby, pushed its hat
down firmly on
its head,

then carried it as inconspicuously
as possible into the school.

3
Witch-Art

It was time for Art. So far Mrs Larkin
hadn't noticed a thing!
The tables had been pushed
together, and
Mrs Larkin had
got the painting
equipment out of the

cupboard and had handed out paint and mixing bowls, paintbrushes and water. It was time for the 'Paint Your Favourite Toy' project. Everybody pulled up their chairs and started to work.

The toys for the project were sitting on the table, together with the paints and water jars.

Sophie propped up the Witch-Baby
in front of her, anchoring its shawl
ends under the water jar. The Witch-
Baby was proving useful – Sophie had
left in such a muddle she'd
forgotten all about bringing a toy from
home.

The Witch-Baby sat on Sophie's
table, taking up rather a lot of room.
It kept grunting and sniffing. The
children were supposed to be
concentrating on their work, but they
kept glancing rather nervously at the
Witch-Baby. They couldn't work out
exactly what it was.

After a few minutes of sitting still,
the Witch-Baby yawned, as if it was
bored. It opened its curious eyes as
wide as they could go, so that its
sparse tufty eyebrows quite
disappeared under the brim of the hat.
Then it twisted its head round and
glared at the paintpots in the middle
of the table.

At once, the painting equipment began to behave in a peculiar manner. The paintpots started to joggle and jig, gently at first, and then more wildly. The paintbrushes took on a life of their own. They began to jump in and out of the paintpots and the water jars, twitching between the children's fingers, and started to do big splashy paintings.

Wild paintings!
Paintings
like you'd never
seen before. But
all the smears and
blodges and stripes and
splatters gradually turned
into pictures that were not
of dolls, or action men, or big
pink elephants, or lorries . . . oh no!
they were all pictures of . . . WITCHES!
Big witches, little witches, witches in
windmills and in wheelbarrows,
witches driving fire
engines or swooping
through caves – all shapes
and sizes of witches, flying
and dancing and casting spells and
generally carrying on!

2 hot

Suddenly the Witch-Baby closed its eyes and yawned, and then it toppled over *thump!* sideways, knocking over Sophie's water jar and several pots of paint.

'What on earth is going on?' cried Mrs Larkin, who had been looking for some felt tips in the cupboard.

Sophie quickly snatched the Witch-Baby off the table, wrapped its shawl right round it so that only its nose and its closed eyes and its hat were visible, and set it down out of sight beside her chair.

The things on the table had stopped jiggling about. The children looked down in astonishment at their pictures. This wasn't at all what they had been meaning to paint!

Mrs Larkin stared at the paintings.

'What is all this! This is chaos! These aren't portraits of your favourite toys! All the same, they are magnificent pictures, so full of energy and inspiration. I don't know what's

come over you all today. Well done!'
Then she looked a bit more closely.
'But all the same, aren't they a
bit . . . ?'

'Witchy?' said Sophie, innocently.
('Verra verra verra witcheeeee!'
murmured the baby, from
down on the floor.)

'Just the word – witchy!'
agreed Mrs Larkin. 'Oh well,
I suppose last night *was*
Halloween. You'll have
heads full of such
nonsense.'

Verra verra verra witcheee

She peeled a swab of paper off a
kitchen roll and started dabbing away
at the spilt paint. 'My goodness, there
are puddles of this green everywhere.
I think we'd better clear up Art now
and get ready for Maths. You can put
your wet pictures out flat beside the
radiator. We'll hang them up when they
are dry.'

Sophie managed to clear up her bit
of table. Then she picked up the
Witch-Baby. 'You've got to behave,'

she whispered. 'This is school, not a
playground. You've just got to be nice
and quiet for the rest of the day.'

'Nicee, softee,' agreed the baby,
sneezing slightly. It looked good as
gold, wrapped in the cobwebby shawl.

All the same, Sophie was beginning
to feel a bit alarmed!

4
The Peacock

Sophie was struggling with her sums.
The Witch-Baby was lying curled up
near Sophie's feet, as if it was a little
dog. For a while she almost forgot it
was there.

Then she became aware of a
muttering:
'Mummmm, mummmm,
mummmm. Hullaballoo
in a balloo. Minnight,
minnight in
a balloo!' burbled
the baby.
'Sssssh!' hissed Sophie.

mummm, mummm, mummmm

Mrs Larkin looked up from the books she was marking: 'Did you say something, Sophie Starling?'

Sophie nudged the baby, but its burblings just got louder. The other children began to giggle. Mrs Larkin went rather pink with annoyance.

'What is that peculiar noise?' she said. She got up and put her ear to the heating pipes, and jiggled the radiator tap.

She opened the window and peered
out, then pulled her head back in,
frowning, forgetting to close the
window even though it was
foggy outside.

'Sophie, that racket is
definitely coming from
your direction.'

'Maybe it's my tummy
rumbling,' said Sophie.
'I only had cola and
cake for breakfast.'

'Well, you should have a proper breakfast like normal people!' said Mrs Larkin, sitting down again at her desk. 'Porridge is very good for stopping tummy rumbles.'

Sophie picked up the Witch-Baby, bounced it around in her arms, then whispered in its small, pale-green ear:

'I told you, you must be quiet.'

'Thassa crosspatch!' hissed the Witch-Baby, wriggling its face free from the shawl and gazing at Mrs Larkin.

'She's nice usually,' said Sophie. 'She's just cross today because the green paint made such a mess on the floorboards.'

But the baby would not be quiet. 'Thassa nitwit!' it said. 'Thassa birdbrain!' And it opened its big goblin eyes as wide as they would go and stared in the direction of Mrs Larkin.

Suddenly, to everyone's amazement, a big greeny-blue bird with a long tail hopped up on to the window-sill and stared into the classroom. The children were so astonished that, instead of calling out, they all drew in their breath.

'Just get on with your sums,' said Mrs Larkin, without looking up. 'I want you to finish this exercise before dinnertime.'

The bird on the window-sill stared
at the class with its small sharp eyes;
then with one big fluttering jump it
flew over to land smack on the top of
Mrs Larkin's head, with its beautiful
tail streaming down behind.

'Thassa peacock!' whispered the
Witch-Baby triumphantly. 'Thassa
big, bad peacock so there, ha ha ha!'

Feeling
quite dizzy
with shock,
Sophie stared
at the bird. The odd
thing was that Mrs Larkin
didn't seem to feel the weight of the
peacock at all, as it sat upon her head.
She just wriggled her neck a bit, and
scratched at her hair absent-mindedly
with the tip of her biro. The children
were all gawping at the peacock. Some
of them giggled, some of them looked
a bit scared.

'If you keep *on* making such a noise,
I'll take your favourite toys and lock
them in the Confiscations Cupboard,'
warned Mrs Larkin.

The bird started to pluck at her hair,
picking up strands with its bill and
pulling.

'Ow!' shrieked Mrs Larkin. 'Eeek!'
She batted at her hair.

'Perhaps yer dog's given yer fleas!'
shouted somebody from the back of
the class.

'You cheeky boy!'

Mrs Larkin was being driven frantic.
She just didn't realise that a great
peacock was sitting on top of her head,
as calm as if it was sitting on top of a
dungheap in a farmyard. Sophie
thought: 'You'd think she'd feel the
weight!' But then she remembered how
the Witch-Baby itself was light as a
pillow to pick up. Maybe this peacock
was itself a kind of Witch-Bird!

'Ugh!' went Mrs Larkin. 'I don't know what's the matter with me this morning. My scalp feels as if it's on fire!' She started to itch and scrape at her head, making the peacock move its legs up and down to escape her fingers. The children stared at her, sitting there wriggling with the peacock on top of her head. Nobody said a word. They wanted to see what would happen next.

Mrs Larkin jumped to her feet and ran to the door. Just before she reached it, the peacock flew up and landed on top of the bookcase; but Mrs Larkin was in such a state she didn't notice that her head had returned to normal. She batted at her mussed-up hair and shouted:

'I'm going to fetch the headmaster. Something mad is going on!'

5
Chaos in the Canteen

The peacock started to fly round the
classroom, its great tail sweeping
books off people's tables and knocking
chalk and pencils on to the floor. It
overturned a jar of dried grasses and
knocked skewwhiff
a picture called
'Our Harvest Festival'
before landing
back on the
window-sill.

At that moment several things happened all at once: the dinner bell rang; the headmaster, Mr Carnforth, threw open the door, and the peacock, with a high-pitched cry, launched itself off the window-sill and disappeared into the fog beyond.

Mr Carnforth gazed at the chaos.

'What has got into this class? The whole place is in an uproar!'

'I'm dreadfully sorry, Mr Carnforth,' said Mrs Larkin, creeping into the room behind him. 'I just don't *know* what's got into everything this morning. The place seems jinxed!'

The headmaster flapped his hands
at the children.

'Clear up this mess, then just go off
and have your dinner. And I don't
want any more trouble. This classroom
is a disgrace!'

He shivered, then strode over and
shut the window with a bang.

'Man is cuckoo!' whispered the
Witch-Baby.

Sophie shivered. She didn't want
cuckoos to add to the confusion. She
cleared up the mess round her place,
then picked up the baby and hurried
off to the canteen.

They still did cooked dinners at
Sophie's school: sausages and beans
and salad and chips and pizzas and
quiche and so on. Sophie didn't ask
the Witch-Baby what it wanted, she
just got herself a plate of beans and
bacon and some bread, then went to
sit down.

The Witch-Baby wriggled around

and tried to sit on the formica table.
Annie, one of Sophie's friends, said:
'I know it's a secret and that, but you
shouldn't have a real baby at school.
Where's its mother?'

'Its mother's a w . . .'

'A what?'

'Away!' said Sophie. 'She's coming
back tonight.'

'Why can't somebody else look after
it?'

'Oh, mind your own business, Annie
Stokes!'

The Witch-Baby extricated its top
half from the shawl, and pointed at
Sophie's plate. It began to scowl.
Sophie tried to feed it some beans on
a plastic teaspoon but the baby
spat out the beans in disgust.

It stood up on Sophie's lap and pointed to the counter where the food was being served:

'Fud fud! Cock-a-leekie! Slurp slurp!' it crowed.

At that very moment, one of the dinner ladies dropped a tin box full of steaming hot sausages and gravy on to the floor and started screeching:

'Yuk! It's full of swarmy things!'

All the other dinner ladies started yelling:

'Look, there's slugs in the lettuce, dozens of them!'

'Look at those quiches. I'm telling you, those wriggly bits, they're never peppers, they're *alive*!'

'This soup looks like it's got ...
BEETLES in it!'

The whole canteen disintegrated
into pandemonium.

The Witch-Baby sat down with a
thump on Sophie's lap.

wriggly squiggledy
higgledy piggledy

it said. 'Is not beetles, is
cockacockacockroaches, ha ha!'

A horrible mixture of gravy and soup
started to ooze under the food counter.
Mr Carnforth came storming in, and
slipped right down in the gunk.

'I don't know what's the matter with this school. This isn't April Fools' Day, there's no excuse!' he stormed. 'If this goes on I'll have to call the police. Get out of the canteen, everybody!'

Poor Mr Carnforth! His trousers were ruined, his elbows were dripping gravy!

The children left their half-eaten meals and ran out into the misty playground, whilst the dinner ladies went off to hunt for bottles of disinfectant and buckets and mops, and Mrs Larkin went off to phone for the pest controller.

Everybody was so surprised at what had happened, they forgot to grumble about not finishing their lunch.

But only Sophie guessed what had *really* been the cause of all the confusion.

She huddled by the railings, trying to keep out of the way of everybody. But then suddenly a whole gang of bigger boys loomed up and surrounded her. The biggest of them, Jimmy Swagger, pushed Sophie, then snatched the Witch-Baby out of her grasp, hollering:

'What are you hiding there, let's see, come on now, let go of it, Sophie Starling!'

6
Piggy-in-the-Middle

The big boys roughly unwrapped the Witch-Baby. Its shawl and pointed hat were thrown down on to the asphalt.

How small and peculiar the poor little Witch-Baby looked, in its green and starry baby-clothes, with a quiff of reddish-green hair that stuck up along the top of its head like a Mohican haircut.

'What a beautiful creature!' said Jimmy Swagger sarcastically. 'What a doll! It's just like a real baby!'

'Do you think it cries like a real baby?' said another of the boys. 'Let's try it out!'

They started to hurl the baby about between them, chucking it topsy-turvy, making its big eyes almost bulge out of its head.

'Give it me back!' screamed Sophie, running desperately between them and trying to snatch the Witch-Baby back. It was as if they were all playing piggy-in-the-middle, with the Witch-Baby as the ball. Higher and higher Sophie jumped, trying to reach it, but in vain. She was terrified it was going to fall.

But then something
odd started to happen. The
baby, instead of hurtling
through the air like a
bundle of rags,
started to float like a gull.
It spread out its small
arms and cried out:

Wheeeeee!!!

and

Peep - peep - peep

and actually seemed to enjoy flying
through the air.

'You come here!' shouted Sophie,
managing at last
to grab the baby

as it executed a sideways swoop.

The baby was shivering all over in excitement.

'You shouldn't have done that!' shouted Sophie at the boys.

'Oh get lost, Sophie Starling!'

The Witch-Baby, which was quite

out of puff, lifted its head and glared at the boys. A small scowl screwed up its face, and it opened its eyes wide and stared at their big boots with a fierce look.

'You give us it back, we was having fun!' said Jimmy Swagger, lunging once more at the baby. But Sophie pushed him back; then, picking up the fallen hat and shawl, she began to run away as fast as she could in the direction of the bike shed.

She was expecting to hear their feet pounding over the playground, but instead she heard a rumpus, and then loud laughter. She slowed down and looked over her shoulder.

Through the mist, she saw the whole group of big boys that had been tormenting the Witch-Baby sitting in a tangle on the asphalt. They were examining their knees, and rubbing their elbows and noses. Sophie moved closer to see what had happened, and then burst out laughing herself. She could see that all their boot-laces had somehow or other

got tied in an enormous knot, so that
as soon as they had started to run
they'd tripped and fallen flat on their
faces, all over each other. Round
them, a crowd of younger children
stood, pointing and mocking.

The Witch-Baby gave a little crow
of triumph.

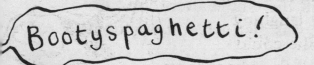

Bootyspaghetti!

it shouted in delight.

7
Noise!

The baby slept for the rest of the
school day. All the same, things still
seemed a bit haywire. Books came
hurtling out of bookcases; Mrs Larkin
got stuck in the stationery cupboard;
and the electric lights kept flicking
on and off the whole afternoon.

Sophie was glad when it was time to
leave.

'What an . . . original-looking doll
that is, Sophie,' said Mrs Larkin as

everyone got ready to go home. 'Who gave you that, then?'

'Dunno, Mrs Larkin.'

Mrs Larkin shook her head: 'Funny girl. Run along home, then. And let's hope tomorrow there are fewer catastrophes than today. It's really been very strange.'

'Ta-ra, Mrs Larkin.'

'Goodbye, Sophie. And take care of your doll.'

As Sophie came back up Cairo Street she could see a light on in the front room. She pushed open the front door and hesitated in the doorway, listening; then quickly she ran upstairs and bundled the sleeping Witch-Baby into her bed with two other dolls and a Kermit frog for company. Then she ran downstairs to say hello to her mother and father.

Her father was cooking the supper
while her mother sorted through some
notes to do with her work that evening.

'Hello, Sophie? Had a good day at
school? I suppose you were late as
usual.'

'I was hours and hours early, I was
there by moonlight,' said Sophie,
knowing they would think she was
joking.

Suddenly, from upstairs, there came
a raucous YELL!

The Witch-Baby!

'Hold on a minute!'

Sophie ran upstairs and turned her radio on really loud. 'Oh do please be quiet,' she pleaded with the Witch-Baby, which opened its big mouth and gaped at her like a fish.

Sophie ran downstairs again. Her mother and father were both frowning meaningfully at the ceiling.

'I thought you'd gone upstairs to turn it down, but it's twice as loud as before, for goodness' sake!' said her mother.

'Can I eat upstairs in my own room, please?'

'Whatever for?'

'There's a programme I want to listen to.'

'It's so loud you could listen to it from down here. You could probably listen to it if you were sitting in a deckchair in New South Wales,' said her father.

'*Please!*'

'Oh all right, Sophie. But turn that caterwauling down!'

Sophie's dad ladled her out some macaroni cheese and a piece of chicken. Sophie managed to smuggle on to her supper tray a glass of milk and some chocolate biscuits and a tin of rice pudding for the baby. She put her old plastic beaker with the funny spout in her pocket, together with a tin opener; then she went upstairs to her room. She tried to feed the screaming Witch-Baby but it wouldn't eat a thing!

It munched everything it was given
into a globby paste, which it then spat
out all over the duvet. It gesticulated
furiously at the tray and cried out:

'Gree gree! Thassa no gree!'

'Oh, baby! What on earth do you
want!'

She felt desperate. The baby's face
started to crumple into a big hiccupy
sob.

'Grease? You want *grease*? No?
Greek? You want Greek yoghurt, is
that it?'

'GREEEEE . . .*N*,' said the baby,
making a great effort.

'Oh,' said Sophie, 'you want
something *green*?'

'Yiss yiss yiss! Gree fud!'

Sophie thought a bit. You'd never get cabbages or sprouts at this time of the evening, all the green-grocers were shut, and the corner shop only sold tomatoes and bananas.

Suddenly she had a brainwave!

But would it work?

She ran downstairs to the kitchen. Her mother and father were eating their food in the front room while they listened to their quiz programme. Sophie rummaged through the food cupboard until she found a little glass bottle: *Green Food Colouring* it said on the label. She slipped it into her pocket and ran upstairs.

The duvet had fallen on to the floor.
The Witch-Baby had got hold of the
Kermit and was chomping at one of its
legs, in between hiccuping with rage.
One of the baby's feet had got caught
in the shawl and had pulled a big
hole in it. The pointed hat was all

squished up beside the pillow.

'I'm coming, baby, I'm coming. Oh
do hush yourself!'

Sophie poured half the little bottle
into the milk, and half into the rice
pudding, then sprinkled the few drops
left on to the chocolate side of the
biscuits.

Immediately the milk and the rice pudding went a dark holly green. The biscuits looked as if they had been scribbled on with felt tip pens.

'Yuk!' said Sophie.

But the Witch-Baby *loved* the green food! It drank all the milk, then slurped down the rice pudding, then licked the green bits off the biscuits. Then it gave a big burp, yawned happily, and lay back in Sophie's arms, smiling sweetly. In two minutes it was sound asleep.

BURP

Sophie watched it carefully, to make sure it didn't turn bright green itself, but its complexion stayed just the same. In its sleep the Witch-Baby sighed contentedly.

'You're a nice little thing, I shall be quite sad to say goodbye,' whispered Sophie.

She laid the baby gently under the duvet, then lay down beside it on top of the bed, her head next to the Witch-Baby's on the pillow. She felt utterly exhausted.

'I'll just close my eyes for five minutes,' she said, turning off the light, 'and then at midnight I'll deliver the Witch-Baby safely back to its mother. I hope!'

8
The Balloon

Sophie was woken by the sound of her
father locking up.

She sat up in alarm. The
luminous hands of the

ZZZZ ZZZ ZZZ ZZZZᶻ

clock said three o'clock.
Three o'clock in the
morning! For a moment
she stared at the clock in
terror. She'd *got* to get the Witch-Baby
back to its mother by midnight! She
couldn't look after it for ever!

Then she remembered that the clock was fast and getting faster.

She jumped out of bed and tiptoed downstairs. The little red light on the television said 23.51. Nine minutes to midnight! There was still just time!

She ran upstairs and picked up the Witch-Baby, wrapped it up tightly, rammed the dented hat back on its head and then crept downstairs holding it in her arms. She ran down the hall and slipped out through the front door, not forgetting to fix the sneck so as to be able to get back in.

She hurried up Cairo Street and turned the corner. As she approached the entrance to Ellison's Scrapyard she heard a far-off church clock begin to strike the hour.

They reached the small pile of bricks just as the chiming ceased.

By now the baby was wide awake. It was quiet, staring with its goblin eyes towards the moon.

'How's she coming then, your Witch-Mummy?' whispered Sophie. 'I don't suppose it's by the All-Night bus! Does she travel by broomstick?'

'Balloo!' said the Witch-Baby, freeing an arm from the shawl and pointing at the sky.

'Yes, just look at the moon!' said Sophie. 'Pretty, isn't it?'

The baby waggled its head.

'No moo, *balloo*!' it said firmly.

Sophie stared up to where the baby pointed, and then she saw it: a small hot-air balloon, with a basket swaying beneath it, slowly, silently, approaching through the air.

'Oh, a balloon!'

'Yiss yiss yiss. Balloo!'

The baby began to tremble with excitement. Sophie heard the faint hiss of jets, and then she saw a young witch in a pointed hat peering over the edge of the basket. Her pale, greeny-white face was half-hidden by cobwebby veils. Her sharp nose was red, as if she had been crying. Beside her Sophie saw the head of a tiny cat, also peeking over the edge of the basket.

The balloon swayed almost overhead.

'Give me back my beautiful baby safe and sound!' called out the witch in a dreamy, singsong voice.

Sophie was so astonished by the arrival of the witch in the balloon that *her* voice came out in a peculiar croak.

'How on earth did you manage to lose your baby?'

'A hotchpotch of misunderstandings and crossed wires, my dear. Halloween does go to our heads, you know. I thought he was safe in his basket, but when I got back home and peered under the shawls, there was the wretched cat. Now I'm back at midnight for my baby, so throw him up, do!'

'I've looked after him all day, all by
myself,' said Sophie. She kept
clutching hold of the Witch-Baby, and
stared up at the witch. 'Where do you
come from?' she asked.

'The other side of Norway and then
some,' shouted down the witch. 'But
I can tell you no more. Now give me
back my baby, I implore you!'

Sophie held out the Witch-Baby, but
the balloon was too far above her head
to reach.

'It's too far!'

'I can't land, it's not permitted outside the hours of Halloween, I'm afraid,' called down the witch, 'so toss him up to me, do! Don't worry, he'll fly like a bird!'

'Promise?'
'Promise!'
'Prommy!' said the Witch-Baby.
So Sophie took in a deep breath.
'Goodbye!' she whispered. 'Safe
journey home!'

Then she tossed the baby into the air, keeping underneath it with her arms open in case anything went wrong. But the baby flew straight up like magic, and landed in his mother's arms.

'Thank you, thank you, you're a good, kind, brave, clever, resourceful kind of a girl,' called the witch.

She leaned over the basket
and threw to the ground
what looked like a handful
of stars. When Sophie bent
down to pick them up she found
they were small silver buttons that
shone in the dark.

She looked back up towards the sky.
The balloon was sailing swiftly away
into the night. Its tiny silhouette
crossed over the moon and
disappeared into the darkness.

Sophie stood for a little while,
staring into the sky; then she turned
and ran all the way home.

'I did very well, looking after the
Witch-Baby,' she said to herself as she
snuggled up under the duvet, with the
silver buttons clutched in her hand. In
less than a minute she was fast asleep.

Sophie went back to being as late for
school as ever, until one day her
mother bought her a proper alarm
clock, with a tea-maker attached, and
a toaster too, so now she can sit up
and eat her breakfast in bed before
she goes to school.

She has a cat now, too, a small black cat who appeared one day in the backyard looking for a home. The cat sleeps on the end of Sophie's bed (though it's not supposed to) and tries to lick the butter off her toast when she's having breakfast. She calls him Cobweb, which reminds her of the Witch-Baby, because of the shawl.

Every year, round about Halloween,
Sophie keeps an eye open, just in case
there are any more Witch-Babies
sitting about waiting to be rescued.
But she hasn't seen one yet!